CAMP SPONGEBOB

by Molly Reisner and Kim Ostrow
illustrated by Heather Martinez

Ready-to-Read

Simon Spotlight/Nickelodeon
New York   London   Toronto   Sydney

Stephen Hillenburg (signature)

Based on the TV series *SpongeBob SquarePants*® created by Stephen Hillenburg
as seen on Nickelodeon®

SIMON SPOTLIGHT
An imprint of Simon & Schuster Children's Publishing Division
1230 Avenue of the Americas, New York, New York 10020

10

Library of Congress Cataloging-in-Publication Data
Reisner, Molly.
Camp SpongeBob / by Molly Reisner and Kim Ostrow ; illustrated by Heather Martinez.— 1st ed.
p. cm. — (SpongeBob SquarePants ready-to-read; #5)
"Based on the TV series SpongeBob SquarePants created by Stephen Hillenburg as seen on
Nickelodeon."—T.p. verso.
Summary: When SpongeBob becomes Sandy's assistant at Bikini Bottom's first summer camp, his
enthusiasm starts to annoy the other staff.
ISBN 0-689-86593-7
[1. Camps—Fiction. 2. Interpersonal relations—Fiction.] I. Ostrow, Kim. II. Martinez, Heather, ill. III. Series:
SpongeBob SquarePants (Television program) IV. Title. V. Series.
PZ7.R27747 Cam 2004   [E]—dc22   2003017679

"As a good assistant, I request permission to check on everyone to make sure they are practicing their duties."

"Go for it, SpongeBob," said Sandy.

First SpongeBob went to Patrick's
rock. He watched quietly as Patrick
practiced the art of sleeping.
Then SpongeBob blew his whistle.
Patrick jumped up.
"Just making sure you are working
hard," explained SpongeBob.
"Now go back to sleep!"

Next SpongeBob peeked
inside Squidward's house.
"I can't hear you," sang SpongeBob.
"Practice makes perfect."

SpongeBob went back to see Sandy,
who was working on her karate moves.
"All counselors are working hard,"
reported SpongeBob.
"Now what should I do?"

"Take a load off and have some
    lemonade," suggested Sandy.
"No time for lemonade,"
    said SpongeBob. "As your assistant,
    I am here to assist.
    How can I assist?"

"Listen, little buddy," said Sandy.
"You are acting nuttier than a bag
  of walnuts at the county fair.
  This camp is supposed to be fun."
"I will make sure it is fun!
  With my assistance, this will be
  the best camp ever!" SpongeBob said,
  cheering.

"Attention, counselors, please
report to me right away,"
SpongeBob said. They all ran to him.
"Now go back to your posts and
PRACTICE! Camp opens tomorrow."

That night SpongeBob was so
excited, he could not sleep.
He decided to visit all
the counselors just to make sure
they were ready.

It was a perfect summer day
in Bikini Bottom. Sandy spent
the morning practicing her new
karate moves.
"Hiiiyaaaa! All this sunshine
makes me more energetic
than a jackrabbit after a cup
of coffee," she said.

"Hey, Sandy, where did you first
learn karate anyway?"
SpongeBob asked.
Sandy told her friend about her days
at Master Kim's Karate Camp.

". . . and I won the championship!"
Sandy finished breathlessly.
SpongeBob leaped in the air.
"Camp sounds amazing!" he shouted.
"But I never got to go."

"When I was little, my dream
was to go to camp. But every summer
my parents sent me to Grandma's.
Sometimes I would pretend she was
my counselor, but I am not sure she
was cut out for camp life,"
SpongeBob said, sighing.

"Say no more, SpongeBob,"
   said Sandy. "Let's open Bikini
   Bottom's first summer camp.
   You can be my assistant."
"I can?" asked SpongeBob.
"Yes, and we can get started
   today," said Sandy.
"I am ready!" shouted SpongeBob.

Sandy gathered Squidward and
Patrick to tell them about the camp.
"Oh, please," Squidward said,
moaning. "Camp is for children."
"Exactly!" shouted SpongeBob.
"It would be for all the little
children of Bikini Bottom."

"Hmmm," Squidward thought out loud.
"Perhaps I could teach the
kids around here a thing or two.
Everyone would look up to me."

"That sounds like lots of fun,"
said Patrick. "When I was at starfish
camp, we used to lie around in the sun
and sleep a lot. I could teach
everyone how to do that!"

"I will teach karate!"
declared Sandy, kicking the air.

"Now go on home and practice
what you are going to teach.
Let's meet back here tomorrow,"
said Sandy.

The next day SpongeBob woke up
in the best mood ever.
"To be a good assistant, I need
to make sure I am prepared
with good camper activities,"
he told Gary.
SpongeBob thought of making Krabby
Patties and having bubble-blowing
contests. He imagined whole days
spent jellyfishing.

SpongeBob ran around his house
gathering all the items he needed.
"Whistle! Check. Megaphone! Check.
Visor! Check. Clipboard?"
Gary slithered over
to SpongeBob's bed and meowed.
"Good job, Gary! Check!"

SpongeBob went over to the mirror
and raised his arms. "Camping
assistants need to be strong!"
he reminded himself
as he flexed his muscles.
"Now I am ready!"

SpongeBob ran over
to the treedome.
Sandy was chopping
wood with her bare hands.
"SpongeBob SquarePants reporting
for duty!" he said, blowing his
whistle three times.

"Squidward," he whispered.

Squidward was fast asleep.

SpongeBob blew his whistle.

"Just making sure you are all
set for tomorrow."

"You are killing me, SpongeBob,"
said Squidward, and he went
back to sleep.

The next morning a very annoyed
Squidward and sleepy Patrick
headed over to Sandy's treedome.
"What are we going to do about
SpongeBob?" asked Squidward.
"I refuse to be ordered around
by him anymore."

"I have just the thing
  for the little guy," said Sandy.

"To express our gratitude
for all your hard work, we have a
small present for you," said Sandy.
"For me?" asked SpongeBob.
SpongeBob opened the box.
Inside was a camp uniform.

"We would like you to be the very
first camper," said Sandy.
"But don't you need me to work?"
asked SpongeBob.
"Nope. We were all so busy preparing
for camp that we never advertised
for campers! You are our first
and only camper!" exclaimed Sandy.

SpongeBob put on his uniform.
"SpongeBob SquarePants
reporting to camp!" he shouted,
running to his counselors.
"I am ready!"